The BOSTON Box

Written by
Carmelita McGrath

Illustrated by
Rochelle Baker

Happy Reading,
Carmelita McGrath

Tuckamore Books
a Creative Publishers imprint

St. John's, Newfoundland and Labrador
2003

©2003, Carmelita McGrath

Le Conseil des Arts | The Canada Council
du Canada | for the Arts

We acknowledge the support of The Canada Council for the Arts for our publishing program.

We acknowledge the financial support of the Government of Canada through the Book Publishing Industry Development Program (BPIDP) for our publishing program.

Cover Art: Rochelle Baker
∞ Printed on acid-free paper

Published by
TUCKAMORE BOOKS
an imprint of CREATIVE BOOK PUBLISHING
a division of Creative Printers and Publishers Limited
a Print Atlantic associated company
P.O. Box 8660, St. John's, Newfoundland and Labrador A1B 3T7

First Edition
Typeset in 14 New Baskerville

Printed in Canada by:
PRINT ATLANTIC

National Library of Canada Cataloguing in Publication

McGrath, Carmelita, 1960-
        The Boston box / written by Carmelita McGrath ; illustrated by Rochelle Baker

ISBN 1-894294-55-6

        I. Baker, Rochelle, 1965- II. Title.

PS8575.G68B69 2003   jC813'.54   C2003-903007-5
PZ7

In memory of the women who
made fish and stories
and for Leah, Molly and Andrea
— may your dream ships sail.
- CM

With buckets of love
for Annie, the sparrow,
Greta, the spur,
and Patrick, the spark.
- RB

It was the hottest summer.

In June, the capelin came in silver waves.
Mary was thrilled, and she raced with her younger sister
Annie to the beach.
They caught the capelin in their nets and scooped them
from the sand.
Silver scales like pieces of moon clung to their hands.
Then they watched the whales that had followed the
capelin into the bay.
The moon was rising, bright as a copper, when they left.

Mary dreamed of copper and silver.

The bright ocean was filled with fish.

And when she dipped her net and lifted it, it was filled with coins.

"Annie, Annie, help me lift all the money!" she called out.

"Dreaming about being rich again," Annie muttered. "Now stop your fancying and let me get some sleep."

In the morning they spread the capelin in the garden, and dug them in. The fish would swim to the roots of the vegetables and make them strong. There would be potatoes — reds and blues — turnips, carrots, cabbages, onions, peas. Mary thought of a dish of buttered peas and she got so hungry she had to run to the house for bread and molasses.

There had been a lot of hunger that year, but everyone said it was over now. The fishermen read the sky and the ocean, and all the signs were right. There would be fish for food and fish to sell to Spain and Portugal and the West Indies. Sometimes, Mary dreamed of sailing a boat to Spain and selling fish to a handsome merchant who filled her open hands with gold.

But girls did not sail boats in that time and in that place. They worked on shore. Mary was twelve and this was her first summer working with her mother and the other older girls and women. They spread codfish on the flakes to dry in the sun, turned it so it dried evenly, and rescued it from the damp when it rained. Annie was nine, still too young to work with them, and she'd been sick all winter, so she minded the babies and sewed and got well.

Mary had to bend and lift, bend and lift, all day. The sun baked her skin. Her hands grew stiff. All she could think of was how good Sunday would be, swimming in the river and reading on the riverbank and eating potato salad. Her great-aunt in Boston had sent some fashion magazines. Mary and Annie would run their hands over the pictures of dresses from Paris and imagine they could feel with their fingers and palms: silk and beads, braid and velvet.

"She's a grand worker, that Mary. She never complains at all," a woman said to Mary's mother.

And Mary didn't complain. She was thinking of the money she'd get in the fall for her share of her family's work in the fishery. She knew she wouldn't really get money, only credit for things she wanted at the store. But that was all right. There would be plenty. Every day her father's boat was laden with cod.

Sometimes she went to the store and looked around to see what she might get.
She passed the jiggers and lamp mantles and stovepipes and went right to the back.

That was where the treasures were.

Calico for dresses, and lace and ribbons to trim them.

Patent leather shoes.

A brooch with a green stone in the middle.

Hair combs glistening with rhinestones shining like trapped raindrops.

She wished she had the nerve to ask the store owner to buy some silk for dresses like they had in Paris. But Mrs. Aggie Jim always looked crooked. And Mary couldn't figure out why a woman would be crooked when she worked all day in a room full of treasures.

"Now what would you be wanting?" Mrs. Aggie Jim asked now in a loud voice.

And all Mary could think of to say was, "Half a pound of sweet biscuits, please."

All summer as she worked, Mary dreamed.

She dreamed of herself in a silk dress trimmed with lace and tiny beads.

She dreamed of her feet in patent leather shoes.

She dreamed of her hair piled high and held with rhinestone combs and emerald ribbons.

She dreamed of herself at a dance and Mrs. Clancy's nephew was out from Placentia and whirling her around in a set of the lancers.

After the dance, he bowed and said, "You're the finest I ever saw."

And she said, "Thank you, Johnny."

And then he said, "Would you like to sail to Spain with me on my ship?"

And she said, "I would. And I will steer the ship while you sleep."

And then she jumped and blushed for her mother was saying, "Stop that lollygagging, Mary. Sure you knows Prince Charming himself'll be out for the garden party."

Annie was singing:
    Mary is a dreamer.
    For sure she is a schemer.
    A fancy dress and a fella to wed
    And sail away on a steamer.

"Get away, Annie, I'm reading." Mary took a smack at her with the magazine, but Annie was already running away laughing among the flaggers by the river.

The copper moons came and went, the breezes grew sharper and summer ended. Her father went to the store to settle up for the fish he'd caught and the work they'd all done.

"Bad news," he said at supper. "The price went down."

"What does that mean?" Mary asked.

"There won't be much left over after we pays the bills. That's what that means."

"But it's grand fish, top grade," her mother said.

"Don't matter when the price is down though, do it?" her father said.

There was not enough left over for silk that year. Or beads or ribbons. There was enough for food and the supplies needed to fish again next year. Her father got himself enough twine to last through a whole winter of mending nets. Mary and Annie got sensible shoes and new coats. Mary hated the clunky shoes. You couldn't dance in them. Their mother got herself a pair of hard boots and a hoe.

"That's what work is for, my girl," she said to Mary. "Work is for getting you geared up for more work. No mistake about it. Stay in school and go off and train for a teacher if you wants anything else."

In the deep autumn night, Mary dreamed.

She dreamed she was sailing the world in a boat loaded with fish.

She would not sell it for a low price, and certainly not to any crooked storekeepers in Newfoundland.

And when she met the handsome Spanish merchant again, he told her she was right. "There are those who will set the prices low, my dear, when the fish come in abundance. You are right to travel the world for a fair price."

And he flooded her open hands with gold.

One day Mary came home from school to see a huge box sitting on the daybed. "Is that the Boston box?" she said.

"It is. Aunt Chrissie's after sending us her old rags again. Rags and tatters and stuff not fit for mortals. Stuff she don't want no more."

Aunt Chrissie sent them a box every Christmas.

"There might be something good in it."

"And I'm the Pope if there is," her mother said and shook her head.

They had a good time unpacking the Boston box, though. It was always good for a laugh. Aunt Chrissie was rich but she sent the strangest things.

There was a spoon too small to be good for anything. "For the elves to eat their jam with," Annie said.

There was a perfume bottle with a tiny bit of perfume in the bottom. "Not enough to baptize a fairy," their mother said.

"A scarf or a doily?" Mary said as she put a scrap of lace on her head.

There were beads that had come off a necklace.

There was one mitten. "Now where's my one-handed child?" their mother said, and pretended to look for him.

They were laughing so hard tears ran down their faces.

24

There was a black mourning gown right to the floor. It looked like it had belonged to a very large lady in another century.

There was a watch, encrusted with red stones but not working.

There was a silvery paper chain of half moons.
"For the January ball when we decorate the palace," Mary said and danced around the room.

There were three unmatched earrings, a spool of brown thread, and a biscuit box full of buttons.

"Tatters and rags," their mother said. "All junk. I told you."

And then she took out a silky lavender dress. A small rhinestone brooch was attached to the front.

"Mine!" Mary said.

Her mother held it out. "I suppose," she said. "You're the one it'd fit."

And below the dress in the box were eight books, more books than they'd ever had in their house before.

The winter was as cold as the summer had been hot, but Annie stayed well that year. And when the other children strapped barrel staves to their feet to go flying down the hills, she was able to go with them. Mary watched her from a warm spot by the window where she sat reading.

The books from the Boston box contained many things that found their way into Mary's dreams. One night she crossed a broad expanse of grassland and saw an African antelope grazing. When she sailed her ship now, she could name all the stars that wheeled above her.

And when she saw the Spanish merchant, she told him she understood much more about the price of fish now, and much more about the world.

"Do you know," she said, "that a war or problems in your country could change the price of fish in mine. Isn't that strange?"

The Spanish merchant said, "You are the most brilliant girl I've ever met. A troupe of fine musicians has just arrived from Barcelona. Would you dance with me?"

She looked at her watch. It was encrusted with red stones and showed her all the time zones of the world.

"I have just enough time," she said, "for one dance before I sail home."